Muddles Puddles and Sunshine

Written by
Diana Crossley

Designed and illustrated by
Kate Sheppard

Hi, this book was written to help you because someone important in your family has died. It can be hard to understand all the things you think and feel when something like this happens. This book will give you some ideas to help you understand what is happening.

Inside you will find lots of helpful activities; some are about the person who has died and some activities are just for fun! Even though someone has died it is still ok to have fun!

Bee will tell you what to do.

Before you start have a good look through this book. Don't feel you have to do the book in the order it is written - you might want to do some bits before others. Ask someone to help you complete the book. First ask them to read the last page as it will tell them how to help you best.

When someone has died things can be very difficult. At times it feels like life is full of MUDDLES and PUDDLES, as well as SUNSHINE moments when you can remember happier times.

I do hope you enjoy it. Fill this book in any way you like. It is yours to keep.

Grown-ups go to the back page.

4

I Want to Remember

Stick a photo here of the person who died.
If you haven't got a photo why not draw a picture and stick it here.

Glue

Write the person's name here.

5

This is Me

Fill this in.

My name is . . . .

I am . . . . . years old

my height is . . .

My eyes are . . .

My favourite colour is . . .

My favourite animal is . . .

My favourite clothes are . . .

This is a picture of Me.

→ THESE ARE THE THINGS I LIKE ←

→ THESE ARE THE THINGS I DON'T LIKE ←

My Family

Draw a picture of your family and answer the questions below.

A PICTURE OF MY FAMILY

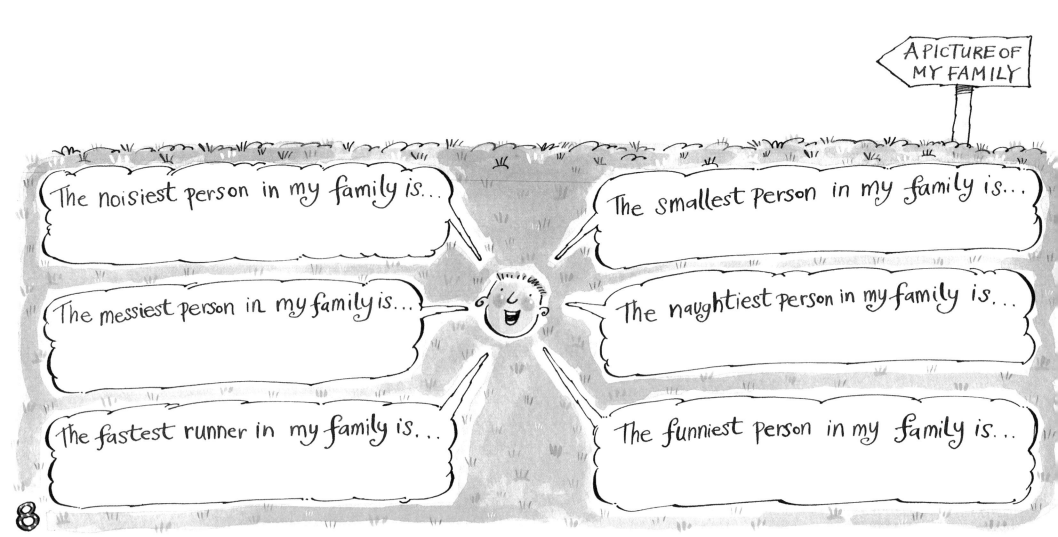

The noisiest person in my family is...

The smallest person in my family is...

The messiest person in my family is...

The naughtiest person in my family is...

The fastest runner in my family is...

The funniest person in my family is...

How to make a Papier-maché spider

This is just for fun.

You will need:
Newspaper
masking tape
flour, water
salt, paint
glue, pen
8 pipe cleaners
paint brush

1 To make the spider's body crumple up some newspaper into a ball shape.

2 Make a smaller ball for the head and tape it to the body using masking tape.

3 Tear up some newspaper into 2.5cm strips.

4 salt   water   flour
Make up a glue from ½ cup of flour, a big spoonful of salt and one cup of water.

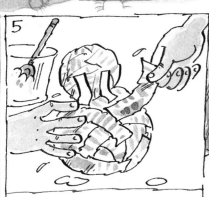

5 Using the flour-glue paste layers of the newspaper onto the head and body. (About 3 full layers).

6 Leave it to dry.

7 When the glue is dry paint the head and body in whatever colour you like.

8 When dry use a pen to punch holes for legs. Put glue on the end of pipe cleaners and stick the legs into the holes in the body.

9 Decorate your spider.

Some people think spiders are scarey. Can you think of any scarey or exciting things you did with the person who died?

9

About the Person Who Died

I have many questions to ask you...

...See if you can fill in the answers below and opposite...

Who died?

What was their name?

When was their birthday?

How old were they when they died?

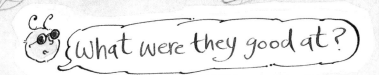 What were they good at?

 What did they look like?

What was their favourite food?

What was the silliest thing the person ever did?

What made the person angry?

 If you don't know the answers to some of these questions, ask someone in your family to help you.

11

How Did They Die?

Write down what you remember or draw a picture that explains how the person died.

How did you find out the person had died? Who told you?

How did you feel?

It is ok to remember the person who died. You might like to light a candle to remember them. Always make sure you do this with a grown-up. Lighting a candle to remember someone in your family who has died can sometimes make you feel sad. It is ok to cry when you feel sad.

13

What Can You Remember About The Person Who Died?

What things did you do together?

What things did they like or not like?

What things don't you like remembering?

The Funeral

When someone dies we have a funeral. Did you go to the funeral?

Yes
What happened?

No
What do you think happened?

Some people choose to visit the grave, or go somewhere special to remember the person. Where do you go to remember the person who died?

15

Feelings Can Be Explosive:

When someone dies you may have lots of different feelings inside you.

MIXED-UP

WORRIED

SAD

ANGRY

People have lots of different feelings when someone dies.
Talking to others sometimes helps. Especially if someone has died in their family too

SCARED

Guilty

Make a

You will need:
A piece of card
paper
glue
sticky tape

4) When it's dry paint your volcano.

I am scared that...

I am angry about...

I get confused when...

I feel lonely when...

Feelings Volcano For Yourself

1. Scrunch up lots of paper into balls about the size of your fist.

2. Get a big piece of card.

3. Start to build up your volcano by sticking the paper balls onto the card.

Use lots of glue and sticky tape.

Now you have a volcano you need to make some explosive feelings *

Make a template in the shape of a spiral then trace lots of spirals onto coloured paper.

When you have lots of spirals complete each of the sentences below onto each spiral.

I'm scared that my friends will bully me

Cut out the spirals and stick them onto your volcano.

I am worried because...

I feel sad because...

I feel excited about...

I feel guilty because....

I Miss Them

When someone in your family dies there may be lots of times you miss them and the things you used to do together.

What things do you miss about the person?
When do you wish they could still be here?

What things might happen to you in the future when you might miss the person who died?

Write a list OR draw pictures

It is normal to miss someone who has died.

Who Is There For Me?

When somebody dies you can feel very lonely. Sometimes it feels like there aren't any people who care, or that there are not enough people to talk to. There are people in your family, friends, at school or clubs, who do care. It can be a good idea to remind yourself who these people are by making your own friendship bracelet.

Follow these instructions to make a fabulous friendship bracelet.

People who care about me...

1

2

3

4

5

6

1 Make a list of six different people who care about you.

2 Choose a different colour thread, yarn or wool for each person on your list. (all the same length).

3 Tie all the threads together at one end.

4 Tape the knotted end to a table.

5 Twist or plait the threads together to make a pattern.

6 Ask someone to help you tie the bracelet around your wrist. Tie a knot in the end.

You could make lots of different bracelets in lots of colours and patterns.

It is ok to miss the person who died, but other people care about you too...

21

Make Your Own Jar of Memories

You will need:

A glass jar with a lid.
Salt
5 coloured chalks
5 sheets of A4 paper
a pen
5 coloured felt tip pens

How to make your salt jar:

1 Fill your jar to the brim with salt.

2 On one piece of paper write down five things you remember about the person who died. These could be things you know they liked, something they enjoyed doing, perhaps somewhere you went together, or what you remember about them as a person.

4 Spread out the other five sheets of paper and divide the salt from the jar between them.

5 To colour the salt take a chalk and rub it backwards and forwards in the salt. The salt will begin to take on the colour of the chalk. The harder you rub the brighter the coloured salt will become.

6 Carefully pick up a piece of paper and pour the coloured salt into the jar one at a time. You can put as much of each colour in as you want. Do this with each pile of salt until the jar is full.

7 When all the colours have been added hold the jar and tap it gently on a work surface to settle the salt. Do NOT shake the jar unless you want all the colours mixed up. Fill in any remaining space with plain salt - right to the very top. This will prevent the colours mixing.

You could draw a picture of your jar of memories here; write down what each colour stands for.

③ Choose a different colour to represent each memory and put a dot of colour next to each memory.

⑧

tap tap

Secure the lid firmly.

My jar of memories for. . . . .

23

Make a Salt Dough Bear

This is just for fun.

You will need: 500g plain flour ○ 250g salt ○ 8fl oz water ○ paint ○ varnish ○

To make the dough...

Mix flour and salt in a bowl.

Add half the water and stir.

Keep adding water bit by bit. Until the dough is firm but not crumbly.

This is the hard part

Knead the dough for ten minutes.

To make a dough bear...

Roll out four bits of dough for the arms and legs.

Take a handful of dough to make the body and flatten it a bit. Then add the arms and legs.

Make a head using a small piece of dough and attach it to the body.

Mark the eyes, nose and mouth with a pencil.

You could also make other dough models of things they liked.

Make some ears and attach them to the head.

Place bear on a tray and bake in an oven for one hour at 145c, 290f, or Gas mark 1·5 Ask a grown-up to help.

You could stick a magnet on the back of the bear. So you can put him on your fridge.

Paint your bear, then when it's dry varnish it. You can make lots of other things in the same way.

24

Make Your Own First Aid Kit

You can make models of these things out of paper, plasticine, clay or Fimo and put them into a box.

What kind of things would you find in a real first aid kit? Make a list.

Now make a list of things that might help you if you have a bad day.

This can be your very own first aid kit.

Playing football.

Patting my dog.

Talking to friends.

Listening to music.

Things that help me.

25

Important Dates

After someone dies you can still remember them, for as long as you want to.

Which dates will you want to remember the person who has died?

Date	Why is it special?

These dates could be days like Christmas, or birthdays, or days when you always went on holiday.

- You could make a calendar, or diary to write these dates in so you remember them.

- You can also ask other people in your family if there are any other special dates. Put these dates in your diary or calendar too.

- On these days you might like to do something special to remember the person who died.....

here are some ideas.....

Go to a place the person liked.

Go to the grave.

Look at some photos.

Light a candle.

Have the person's favourite food for tea.

Other things I can do are....

26

Tremendous Tulips

Sometimes it's hard to think about the future without the person who died. Life will always be different now they have died. There will be times when you are sad, but it's still ok to have good times too.

Write three messages in the boxes below and then copy them onto three pieces of paper.

I wish I could tell you....

One thing I want to do when I'm older is....

A time in the future when I might miss you....

1. Get a terracotta plant pot and decorate it. You can do this with paints or stick shells or small stones onto it with glue.

2. Put some small stones in the bottom of the pot for drainage.

3. Fold up the messages and put them in the pot.

4. Fill the pot over half way with soil or compost.

5. Plant the tulip bulbs.

6. Water the bulbs regularly.

7. Wait for them to grow!

As your flowers grow, they will keep your messages safe. Bulbs are good as they grow again year after year.

27

Fantastic Photo Frame

Looking at photos can help you remember the person who died.

You will need:
A clip frame. paper. glue. felt pens. scissors. stickers. your favourite photo of the person who died.

clips

1 Take the clips off the clip frame and put them aside to use later.

2 Cut out a piece of coloured paper the size of the frame as a background to your photo.

3 Stick your photo onto the coloured paper.

4 Decorate round the sides of your photo with stickers or pictures or words.

5 Clip the frame back together.

Sometimes it is nice to look at photographs of the person who died. Where will you keep your frame?

28

Saying Hello Again

Sometimes people might tell you not to think about the person who died. They think you should only think about the future.

Maybe you have to do both....think about the person who has died and still try to enjoy your life without them.   This isn't always easy.

If you could send a letter to the person who died what would you tell them?

Write a letter to the person who has died and keep it somewhere safe inside an envelope.

You could tell them how you are and what you've been doing. You could say how you felt when they died, you could also tell them about other people in your family, or your wishes

Five More Minutes

If the person who died could come back for just five minutes, what would you tell them?

If you could come back just for five minutes, I would tell you...

Write a message on the tag.

You could write a message on some paper and attach it to a helium balloon, and let the balloon go.

Goodbye

We hope you have enjoyed this book. You may want to show it to other people, or look at it yourself from time to time. Goodbye!

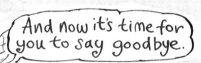

And now it's time for you to say goodbye.

my Memory Box

You can keep this book in a box which can be your memory box. There may be other things you want to put in the box that remind you of the person who died. You might want to share your box with special friends. Goodbye!

This book was completed by...

With the help of...

Today's date is...

This is a picture of me..... and .... ..this is the person who helped me.

And these are our thoughts about the book.

31

Guidelines for Grown Ups

This book tries to help children make sense of their experience following a family death. It was written to help children understand more about their thoughts and feelings when someone important has died. The book could also become a useful store of memories, which can be a source of comfort, especially for a child who is worried they may forget the person who has died.

A child's grief can be hard to comprehend. Unlike adults they tend to 'jump in and out' of their grief, which can seem confusing for the grown ups around them. Children can feel very absorbed by their grief. At other times they appear to carry on life as normal, perhaps unwittingly protecting other family members. They may feel mixed up and confused about issues they do not understand, but feel wary of asking questions, especially if they think their questions may upset grown ups. So, life for a child can seem to be a mixture of 'muddles, puddles and sunshine' after someone important has died.

This book uses a wide variety of activities to reflect the different aspects of grief, whilst also trying to find a balance between remembering and having fun and building a resilient, hopeful future.

Children will need to find an adult who can help them complete this activity book. This has to be someone they trust who they can count on to help them complete the activities over a number of weeks. This could be a parent, although it might be preferable to consider a more distant relative, teacher or friend of the family who may be less emotionally involved. However it is important to encourage the child to share their book with their parent(s) as this may help increase open discussion within the family. Children may like to ask their parent(s) to try out some of the fun 'home activities' with them!

Each child is an individual and you will therefore need to work at their pace. However the book can be broadly divided into 6 sessions, with a fun activity to be completed between sessions. It is useful to ask the child to bring their 'home activity' to the next session for discussion. Sessions will normally require about an hour depending on the age and development of the child.

We hope you enjoy helping a child to create their book. It may be an invaluable keepsake of memories in the years to come.

	SESSION 1	SESSION 2	SESSION 3	SESSION 4	SESSION 5	SESSION 6
PAGES	4, 5, 6, 7, 8 9 for 'home activity'	10, 11, 12, 13, 14, 15 16 for 'home activity'	17, 18, 19, 20 21 for 'home activity'	22, 23 24 for 'home activity'	25, 26, 27 28 for 'home activity'	29, 30, 31, 32

Winston's Wish

- is the leading childhood bereavement charity in the UK
- offers the widest range of practical support and guidance on bereavement to children, their families and professionals
- provides professional therapeutic help in individual, group and residential settings, and via a national helpline, interactive website and publications
- is the only specialist provider of residential group support for children bereaved through violence
- is almost entirely dependent on voluntary donations for its income

The Winston's Wish Helpline (**08452 03 04 05**), staffed by qualified practitioners, provides guidance and information for anyone supporting a bereaved child.

Other publications from Winston's Wish include:

Out of the Blue is an activity book created by Winston's Wish to help teenagers remember the person who has died and to help them express their thoughts and feelings.

32 pages   148 × 210mm   Full colour illustrations
Paperback   ISBN 978-1-903458-71-6   £7.99

A child's grief – supporting a child when someone in their family has died. A useful introduction for any adult supporting a child through bereavement, it covers a variety of issues that may affect a child when a person close to them dies.

32 pages   297 × 210mm   Full colour illustrations   Paperback
ISBN 978-0-9559539-3-4   £5.99

Also from Hawthorn Press:

All the dear little animals by Ulf Nilsson and Eva Eriksson
All the dear little animals is a thoroughly off-beat, charming and whimsical story of three children responding to death.
'*This captivating book takes us on a safe, funny and deeply meaningful adventure.*'
Julie Stokes OBE, Founder and Clinical Director of Winston's Wish.

36 pages   216 × 218mm   Full colour   Hardback
ISBN 978-1-903458-94-5   £9.99
www.hawthornpress.com

Further information and specialised publications can be found on our website – www.winstonswish.org.uk